Craig Kee Strete

LITTLE COYOTE RUNS AWAY

Illustrated by
Harvey Stevenson

G. P. Putnam's Sons   New York

Book designed by Gunta Alexander. Text set in Garth Graphic.

Library of Congress Cataloging-in-Publication Data
Strete, Craig. Little Coyote runs away/by Craig Kee Strete;
illustrated by Harvey Stevenson.   p.   cm.
Summary: Mother Coyote tells Little Coyote to clean his fur before
eating, but since he hates washing, he runs away from home
and uses magic to protect himself. [1. Coyotes—Fiction. 2. Runaways—Fiction.
3. Magic—Fiction.] I. Stevenson, Harvey, ill. II. Title. PZ7.S9164Li 1997
[E]—dc20 95-12604 CIP AC ISBN 0-399-22921-3
2 4 6 8 10 9 7 5 3 1
First Impression

For Wina and John.—H.S.

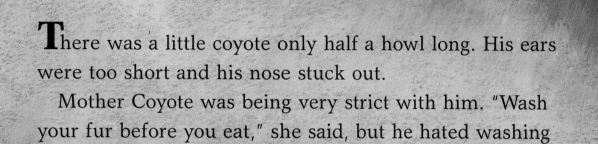

There was a little coyote only half a howl long. His ears were too short and his nose stuck out.

Mother Coyote was being very strict with him. "Wash your fur before you eat," she said, but he hated washing his fur.

"My tongue gets all sticky and I won't do it," said Little Coyote.

"Only clean little coyotes get to eat in this den," said Mother Coyote.

"Then I am running away," Little Coyote said, as he sat in the tall grass beside Mother Coyote's den.

Mother Coyote yawned and covered her mouth with one paw. "Well, if you are going to run away, make sure you take your special medicine bag, Little Coyote. It will protect you against danger," she said.

So Little Coyote went into the den and got his special medicine bag and put his magic things in it.

And then he ran away.

Little Coyote went over the high hill and under the big trees and then he met a green grass-eating giant goat. It had sharp horns and looked big enough to eat a small coyote.

Little Coyote took his magic corn pollen from his medicine bag and sprinkled it on the ground. The grass grew so high the goat couldn't see him.

So Little Coyote crept through the grass and got away.

Little Coyote went over the not-so-high hill and under the not-so-big trees and then he met a black-billed, big-winged buzzard. It sat on a big rock and looked hungry enough to eat a small coyote.

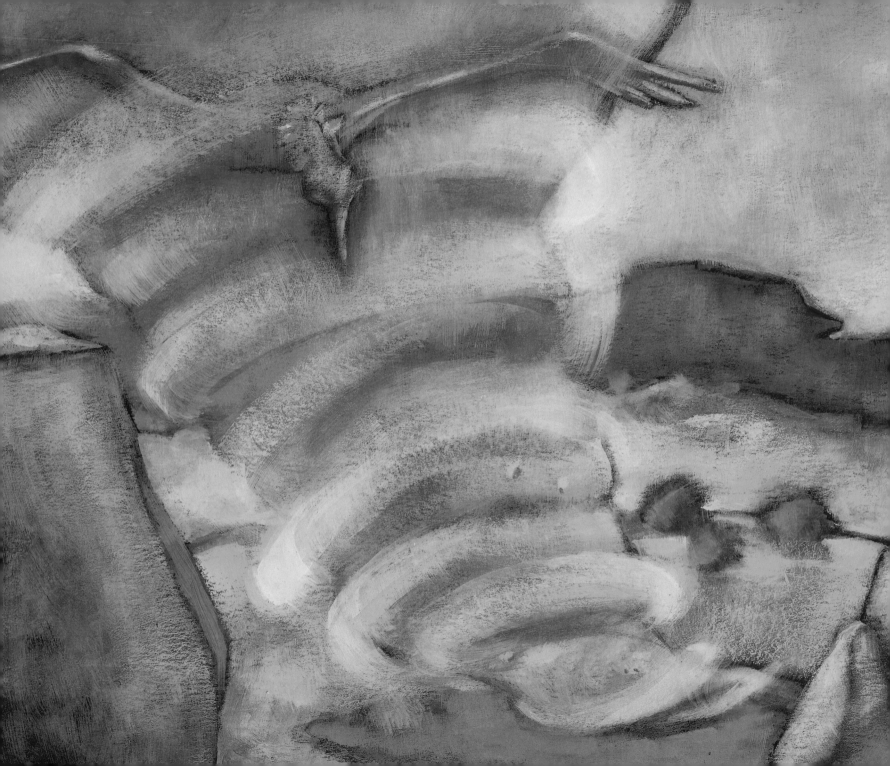

Little Coyote took his magic tobacco out of his medicine bag and blew it into the wind. The wind whirled and twirled and the dust rose up in the air so high the buzzard couldn't see him.

So Little Coyote tiptoed through the dust and got away.

Little Coyote went over ground too small to be a hill
and under trees not much bigger than himself and then
he met a brown-backed, big-toothed bear. It was clawing
a big tree and looked mean enough to eat a small coyote.

Little Coyote took his magic eagle feather out of his medicine bag and shook it in all four directions. It rained in the South and snowed in the West and hailed in the East and dropped icy sleet in the North and the bear was so busy looking at it all he couldn't see him.

So Little Coyote ran through the weather and got away.

Little Coyote had now reached the end of the hills and
the last of the trees and then he met a horde of honking
cars. It was noisy and the cars were going so fast it
looked like they could hurt a small coyote.

Little Coyote reached in his medicine bag and got out a little of each of his magic things and sprinkled them on the ground.

The wind from the speeding cars and trucks blew it all away.

Little Coyote reached in his bag again, but now it was empty. Little Coyote felt very alone.

He thought about his cozy den, his kind mother, and mostly he thought about dinner. Everything suddenly seemed much too far away.

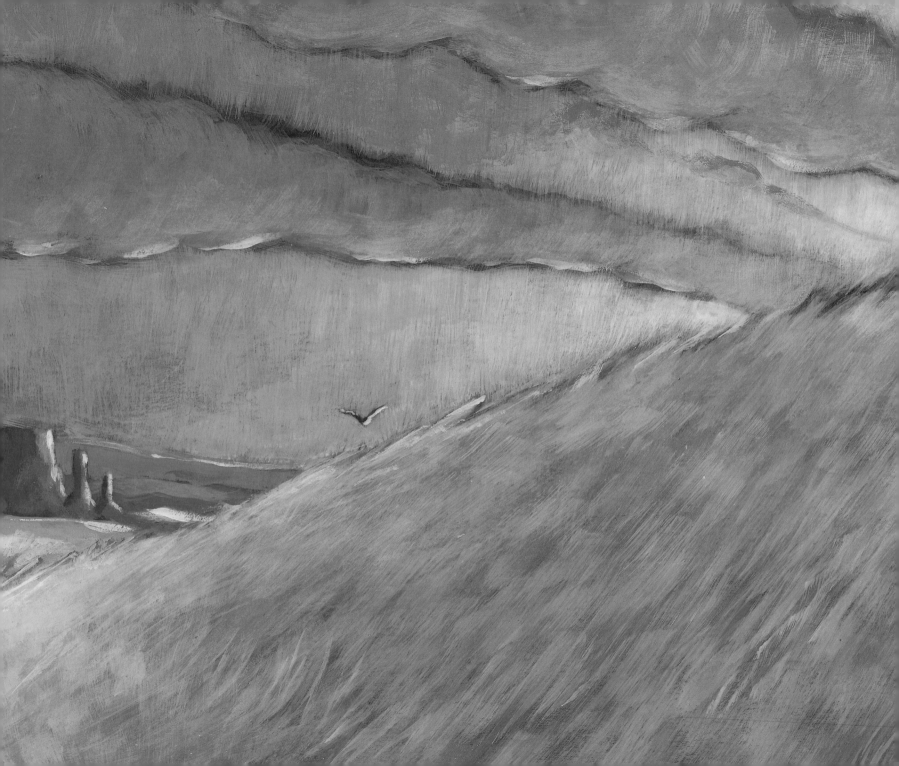

So he turned around and unran away.

Little Coyote trotted over ground too small to be a hill,
over not-so-big hills, and finally ran as fast as he could
back over the high hills.

He yipped with coyote joy when he saw the entrance
to his den.

Mother Coyote had supper ready for him. She seemed
to know he would be back. He cleaned his fur quite
happily before he sat down to eat.

Little Coyote told her all about running away.

"Why did you come back?" asked Mother Coyote.

"I ran out of magic. I had to come back and get some
more," said Little Coyote.

"Was that the only reason you came back?" asked Mother Coyote.

Little Coyote told the truth. "I also missed you. I missed being snug and warm in our den. And I even missed getting clean for dinner."

"There is one magic that always works," said Mother Coyote, and she gave him a big welcome-back hug. "Because home is the magic."

Little Coyote sat happily in his den, safe from goats, buzzards, bears, and horrible highways, and knew it was true.